ISBN: 978-0-9915026-2-2

$9.99
ISBN 978-0-9915026-2-2
50999>

9 780991 502622

Published by Little England Books

Dedicated to Bowie,
who fills our lives with joy every day.

Bo takes naps

And eats his food

Bo licks his foot

And sleeps on his back

Bo wakes up

And Bo has a drink

Bo lies on the couch

In the living room

And Bo looks

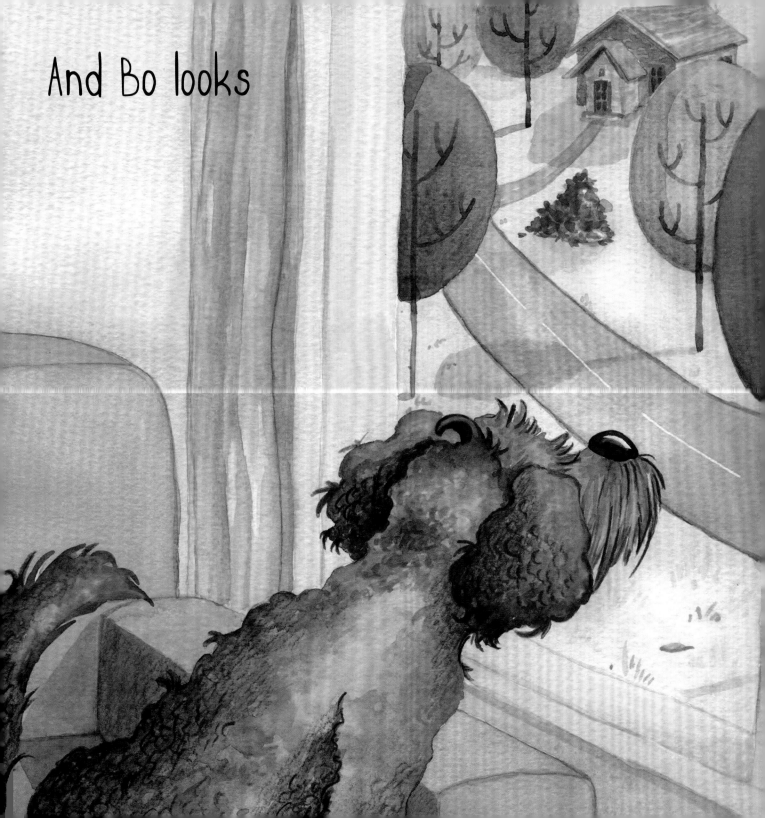

Out at the street

And Bo greets

The delivery men

Then Bo
gets up
and

Paces around

He looks
at us
and

Wants a walk

Because,
sometimes,

Bo gotta go!